For information about permission to reproduce selections from this book, write to Permissions, Houghton Mifflin Harcourt Publishing Company, 215 Park Avenue South, New York, New York 10003.

Library of Congress Cataloging-in-Publication Data is on file.

ISBN 978-0-547-58519-2 pa
ISBN 978-0-547-62913-1 pob
ISBN 978-0-547-59560-3 bilingual

Cover design by Rachel Newborn. Book design by Bill Smith Group.
www.hmhbooks.com
www.marthathetalkingdog.com

Manufactured in China
LEO 10 9 8 7 6 5 4 3 2 1
4500289807

A Winter's Tail

MARTHA HABLA
Perritos en invierno

Adaptation by Karen Barss Adaptación de Karen Barss
Based on the TV series teleplay written by Raye Lankford
Basado en la serie de televisión escrita por Raye Lankford
Based on the characters created by Susan Meddaugh
Basado en los personajes creados por Susan Meddaugh
Translated by Carlos E. Calvo Traducido por Carlos E. Calvo

Houghton Mifflin Harcourt
Boston • New York • 2011

Martha and her friends were watching the hockey playoffs.

"Go, team!" yelled Carolina. Then she noticed Skits cowering nearby. "I think my cheering scared your dog," she said.

Martha y sus amigos estaban mirando las finales de hockey.

—¡Vamos! —gritó Carolina.

Enseguida notó que Skits se acurrucaba en un rincón.

—Creo que mi grito de aliento asustó a tu perro —dijo.

"Skits isn't afraid of cheering. He's afraid of hockey pucks," Martha told her.

"It happened a long time ago," said Helen, "when Skits was still a puppy."

Martha and her friends all remembered that long-ago winter day . . .

—Skits no les tiene miedo a los gritos de aliento. Les tiene miedo a los discos de hockey —le dijo Martha.

—Ocurrió hace mucho tiempo —explicó Helena—, cuando Skits todavía era un cachorro.

Martha y todos sus amigos recordaron aquel día de invierno de hacía tanto tiempo...

That was the day they woke up to a wonderful surprise. A huge snowstorm and no school! Everyone ran outside to play. Everyone, that is, except Skits. He had never seen snow before and he was scared.

Aquel día se despertaron para encontrar una sorpresa maravillosa. Había una tormenta de nieve impresionante... ¡y no había escuela! Todos salieron a jugar. Todos menos Skits. Skits nunca había visto nieve y estaba asustado.

"What do you think, Skitsy?" Helen asked. "This is snow. It's fun!"
But Skits wouldn't budge.

"I know," said Martha. "I'll get Mr. Chewy! He can't resist Mr. Chewy."
And she ran into the house to get the squeaky toy.

—¿Qué pasa, Skitsy? —le preguntó Helena—. Es nieve, nada más. Y es divertido.
Pero Skits ni se movía.

—¡Ya sé! —dijo Martha—. ¡Iré a buscar al Sr. Muérdeme! Con él, Skits no
pondrá resistencia —y se fue corriendo a casa a buscar el juguete que chillaba.

"Skits, look what I've got," Helen said, squeaking the toy as she threw it up in the air.

"Who's going to get Mr. Chewy?" Martha called.

The kids got down on all fours and grabbed at the toy.

—Skitsy, mira lo que tengo —dijo Helena, haciendo sonar el juguete y arrojándolo al aire.

—¿Quién va a agarrar al Sr. Muérdeme? —gritó Martha.

Los chicos se pusieron a cuatro patas y agarraron el muñeco.

SQUEAK
SQUEAK

CUIII
CUIII

"I want Mr. Chewy," said T.D. with a growl.

"No, I want Mr. Chewy," said Alice.

Finally, Skits couldn't resist and he jumped off the step and into the snow.

"Hooray for Skits!" the gang shouted.

—¡Quiero el Sr. Muérdeme! —rezongó Toni.

—¡No! El Sr. Muérdeme es para mí —dijo Alicia.

Finalmente, Skits no aguantó más y saltó del escalón a la nieve.

—¡Bravo por Skits! —gritó la pandilla.

Soon, Alice's brother Ronald appeared with some friends.

"Instead of crawling around like babies, how would you like some real action?" he asked.

"You're on!" replied Alice. "We'll meet you at the lake with our skates."

Enseguida llegó Ronald, el hermano de Alicia, junto con unos amigos.

—En vez de estar gateando como bebés, ¿no les gustaría hacer algo más emocionante? —preguntó.

—¡Trato hecho! —respondió Alicia—. Nos vemos en el lago con los patines.

At Dog Head Lake, the kids set up their hockey rink.
Ronald pointed to a far-off area.

"If the puck lands over there," said Ronald, "it's out of play.
The ice is thin by the stream and it's too dangerous to go after it."

En el Lago Cabeza de Perro, los
chicos hicieron una cancha de hockey.
Ronald señaló el límite.

—Si el disco cae allí —dijo
Ronald— no lo busquen. Ahí cerca
está el arroyo. El hielo es muy
delgado y es peligroso ir a buscarlo.

Alice and Ronald faced off, while Martha, Skits, and Truman watched from the shore. Truman clapped his hands to keep warm.

Alicia y Ronald se pararon frente a frente, mientras Martha, Skits y Truman miraban desde el borde. Truman aplaudía para calentarse las manos.

But when Alice skated past and whacked the puck, Skits couldn't sit still. He took off, chasing after it.

"Skits! No!" yelled Martha. "You'll mess up the game."

But it was too late.

Pero cuando Alicia pasó patinando y le pegó al disco, Skits no pudo quedarse sentado. Salió corriendo detrás del disco.

—¡No, Skits! —gritó Martha—. Vas a arruinar el partido.

Pero ya era demasiado tarde.

Ronald had the puck, but not for long.

Ronald alcanzó el disco, pero no por mucho tiempo.

At first, Ronald was mad. But he changed his mind when he saw what happened next.

"All right!" he cheered, as Skits and the puck slid through the goal markers. "*Your* pup just scored a goal for *our team!*"

Al principio, Ronald se enojó, pero cambió de parecer cuando vio lo que ocurría después.

—¡Eso es! —animó Ronald mientras Skits y el disco resbalaban hacia la portería —. ¡*Tu* mascota acaba de anotar un gol para *nuestro equipo!*

"Sorry, Skits," said Helen after she tied him to a tree. "Here, play with Mr. Chewy."

—Lo siento, Skits —le dijo Helena después de atarlo a un árbol—. Quédate jugando con el Sr. Muérdeme.

But every time the hockey puck went by, Skits pulled on the leash, trying to chase the puck. And every time he pulled, the leash became a little bit looser.

Pero cada vez que el disco pasaba por delante suyo, Skits tiraba de la correa tratando de alcanzarlo. Y cada vez que tiraba, la correa se aflojaba más.

Suddenly the leash untied and Skits was free. He chased the puck past the goal markers and right toward the thin ice!

YIP, YIP, YIP!

"Skits, no! Stop!" yelled Helen.

"Leave it, Skits!" Martha shouted. "Leave it!"

De repente, la correa se soltó y Skits quedó libre. Corrió detrás del disco, pasó por la portería y fue hacia el hielo delgado. *¡Fiuu, Fiuu, Fiuu!*

—¡No, Skits! —gritó Helena.

—¡Déjalo, Skits! —gritó Martha—. ¡Déjalo!

Skits slid to a stop just as a large crack appeared on the ice all around him. The kids gasped.

"Don't move, Skits," said Martha in her most serious alpha dog voice. "I'll get Mom and Dad. They'll know what to do."

Skits patinó. Al detenerse, apareció una grieta enorme en el hielo, que lo rodeaba completamente. Los chicos se quedaron paralizados.

—Skits, no te muevas —le dijo Martha con su mejor voz de perro parlante—. Voy a buscar a mamá y papá. Ellos sabrán qué hacer.

Martha ran home as fast as she could.

"Help!" panted Martha. "Skits is stuck on thin ice!"

With not a moment to lose, Martha and Dad ran back to the lake.

Martha fue corriendo a casa lo más rápido que pudo.

—¡Socorro! —jadeó Martha—. ¡Skits está atrapado en el hielo delgado!

Sin un minuto que perder, Martha y papá fueron corriendo hacia el lago.

"Hurry, Dad," said Helen. "The ice is breaking up!"

Dad tied a rope to the raft. Then he slid the raft toward Skits.

"Okay, Skits," he called. "Climb on."

But as Skits crept forward, the ice cracked again, and he stopped.

—¡Rápido, papá! —gritó Helena—. ¡El hielo se está quebrando!

Papá ató una cuerda al bote inflable. Después deslizó el bote hacia Skits.

—Muy bien, Skits —le gritó—. ¡Súbete!

Pero cuando Skits se acercó lentamente,
el hielo volvió a quebrarse, y se detuvo.

"That ice isn't going to hold him much longer," said Dad. "But how do you get a scared puppy to climb into a raft?"

—El hielo no aguantará mucho —dijo papá—. ¿Cómo lo hacemos para que un perrito asustado se suba al bote?

"I know," said Martha. She ran back to the tree to get Mr. Chewy. "Tie Mr. Chewy to the raft," she told Dad. "Skits can hold on to it, and you can pull him back to solid ice."

—Ya sé —dijo Martha, y fue corriendo al árbol donde estaba el Sr. Muérdeme.
—Ata al Sr. Muérdeme al bote —le dijo Martha a papá—. Así, Skits querrá agarrarlo y tú podrás tirar para traerlo al hielo firme.

Dad tied the squeaky toy to the raft and slid it to Skits.
"Come on, Skitsy," coaxed Martha. "Grab Mr. Chewy."

Papá ató el muñeco que chillaba al bote y lo deslizó hacia Skits.
—Vamos, Skitsy —lo animó Martha—. Agarra al Sr. Muérdeme.

Just as the ice broke off underneath him, Skits lunged at Mr. Chewy and Dad pulled him to safety. Everyone cheered.

Justo cuando el hielo se terminaba de quebrar y se hundía, Skits saltó hacia el Sr. Muérdeme y papá pudo tirar para salvarlo. Todos celebraron.

"And ever since then," Helen said, concluding her story, "Skits has been afraid of hockey pucks."

Carolina scratched her head. "That doesn't make sense," she said. "He should be afraid of thin ice."

"Dog logic," said Martha.

—Y desde ese día —dijo Helena para terminar la historia—, Skits les ha tenido miedo a los discos de hockey.

Carolina se rascó la cabeza.

—Eso no tiene sentido —dijo—. Debería tenerle miedo al hielo.

—Lógica de perros —dijo Martha.

Helen smiled. "It comes in handy," she said. "Now we have a great way to keep him out of the garbage."

Helena sonrió.

—Pero nos resulta útil —dijo—. Ahora tenemos una buena manera de mantenerlo lejos del cubo de basura.

PONDOK MOUNTAIN – SPITZKOPPE

Drenched in the golden light of sunrise, the Pondok Mountain stands near one of Namibia's best-known landmarks, Grosse Spitzkoppe, a granite massif soaring to 1,728 m. Together with the Kleine Spitzkoppe, these mountains are located in the eastern Namib Desert where the rainfall is higher and the vegetation more lush. Natural pools formed by accumulated rainwater can be found at the base of the mountains, providing a home for various creatures such as the Herero chat, an extremely rare indigenous bird species. The first nest of this species' eggs was discovered in the Pondok Mountain. High up in the same mountain is Bushman's Paradise, a large shelter and ancient rock art site.

THE ORGAN PIPES

Over 120 million years ago, surging from deep below the earth's surface, magma moved upwards through a fracture in the sedimentary shales of the Karoo Sequence rock. Solidified by gradual cooling, the magma transformed into dolerite beneath the surface of the earth. Subsequent contracting and cracking split the dolerite into jagged shafts, which were eventually exposed by years of water and wind erosion. This has left a distinctive formation known as the Organ Pipes, near Burnt Mountain. The name is an apt description of the long, narrow shape of the five- to seven-sided perpendicular columns, some of which reach up to five metres.

THE NAMIB DESERT

The Namib Desert stretches along the coast from the Olifants River in South Africa to Namibe in Angola. Confined by the Atlantic Ocean in the west, the desert sprawls inland towards the escarpment which forms its eastern boundary. Each of its three sections has a distinctive ecosystem. The south is dominated by a reddish-orange sea of shifting sand dunes between the Kuiseb and Orange rivers. Between the southern dune sea and the northern Namib are the gravel plains, scattered inselbergs and steep-walled gorges of the central Namib, between the Kuiseb and Huab rivers. The Huab and Kunene rivers form the borders of the northern Namib, which comprises the fog-shrouded Skeleton Coast and the mountainous Kaokoveld.

PARABOLIC DUNES – SOSSUSVLEI

The Namib Desert, with its silent giants of sand and rock, is thought to be the oldest desert in the world. Whilst the dunes probably first formed 40 to 15 million years ago, it is estimated that the desert has been semi-arid to arid for the last 80 million years. These beautiful, curved dunes in the Sossusvlei area are classified as parabolic or multicyclic and are common along coasts where winds blow regularly and where sand is abundant.

SYMPHONY OF SAND

With the assistance of the wind, dunes are usually formed around an obstruction such as vegetation, a stone or even coarse sand grains. Prevailing winds are also the sculptors of the dunes' contours and curves. The winds continuously drive sand particles up the long, wavy dune slope and scatter them into the air, from where the sand drifts back to the slipface – the steep downward face on the leeward side where sand actively cascades. The dune crests are kept sharp by eddies. These circular winds blow from the base of the dune up the slipface towards the crest. They keep the slipface steep and help prevailing winds distribute sand to the surrounding dunes.

LIVING IN A WATERLESS WORLD

At Kolmanskop, once a thriving mining town in the Namib Desert, mine owners paid high wages and granted several fringe benefits to their employees. Every day families would be supplied with free ice, soda water and lemonade. Despite these luxuries, Kolmanskop experienced difficulty in obtaining fresh, drinkable water and the settlement largely depended on barrelled water shipped from Cape Town to Lüderitz. Notwithstanding the complicated logistics of obtaining water, Kolmanskop had a swimming pool fed by sea water pumped from Elizabeth Bay, 35 km south of Kolmanskop. The water was later used in the diamond-washing process. The local hospital, one of the country's finest, was the first in the then South West Africa to get an X-ray machine.

SWAKOPMUND LIGHTHOUSE

Between the cold Atlantic Ocean and the torrid Namib Desert lies Swakopmund, its streets lined with palm trees and brightly-coloured flowerbeds. The town, with a population of approximately 18,000, began life in 1892. With Walvis Bay in British hands, Germany needed an alternative harbour to gain access to the interior of the land it had colonised. The task to find a suitable site fell to Captain Curt von François and the crew of the *Hyäne*. Their search ended near the mouth of the Swakop River, where they erected two beacons to mark the landing site. Soon thereafter, construction began on a harbour, a mole and a jetty. The lighthouse was completed in 1902 and an extra 10 m were added to the 11-metre-high structure in 1910.

WELWITSCHIA MIRABILIS

Endemic to the Namib Desert, the *Welwitschia mirabilis* or 'dwarf tree' is one of the world's rarest plants. With an estimated lifespan of 1,500 years, these 'living fossils' were described by Charles Darwin as the 'platypus of the plant kingdom', having adapted remarkably to the hostile desert climate. Throughout its lifetime, the plant produces a single pair of leaves, which are fibrous and unpalatable for animals. Austrian doctor and botanist, Friedrich Welwitsch, was honoured with the discovery of the *Welwitschia* in 1859, although he was not the first to have encountered the intriguing plant. There is still much debate about its exact classification and scientists regard it as a link between gymnosperms and angiosperms.

FISH RIVER CANYON

It is only towards the end of its course that the Fish River descends into the spectacular Fish River Canyon. Twisting and turning through this mighty chasm, the river is a source of life amidst the vast expanse of bare rock and almost barren canyon walls. The Fish River flows seasonally, but during the rainless months it leaves behind a string of muddy pools in the canyon. Although rarely seen, animals living in this semi-arid environment, such as Hartmann's mountain zebra, klipspringers and Chacma baboons, never stray too far from the riverbanks. The canyon, proclaimed a protected area in 1969, is part of the Fish River Canyon Conservation Area.

QUIVER TREE
FOREST

Northeast of Keetmanshoop, on the farm Gariganus, grows a spectacular forest of about 250 quiver trees. The quiver tree or *kokerboom* is well adapted to harsh conditions, retaining water in its spongy trunk and succulent leaves. The San found the soft and easily hollowed wood of the tree ideal for making quivers, hence the name. The larger specimens have a diameter of one metre at ground level and, though usually between three and five metres high, they can grow up to nine metres. The quiver tree has a lifespan of about 300 years, and displays its first bright-yellow blooms when it is between 20 and 30 years old.

A VANISHING CULTURE

For millennia the only humans in southern Africa were probably the San, a semi-nomadic, hunter-gatherer people. Their lifestyle began to change about 2,000 years ago when a pastoral revolution drove Nguni people into the San's traditional hunting grounds. These pastoralists introduced a new way of life: cattle rearing and crop cultivation. Centuries later, Portugal's search for a sea route to India paved the way for European colonisation of the subcontinent. The newcomers brought firearms, notions of individual ownership and powerful prejudices against southern Africa's 'first people'. Combined, these led to the marginalisation, enslavement and killing of the San. Today few of Namibia's 33,000 San still have access to ancestral land.

ROCK ART

Twyfelfontein, in the Khorixas district, is the site of one of the most spectacular, largest and longest-running outdoor art exhibitions in the world. Its gigantic rock canvases – variously angled, free-standing rock slabs – contain petroglyphs of exceptional variety and quality. These ancient engravings depict a range of animals, spoor, bird clawprints, symbols, patterns and circles. This purple-hued, weather-textured rock shows an 'African centaur' carved intaglio. In places, the red sandstone of this area is interbedded with purple conglomerates, which may have been finely ground in order to colour this artwork. More than 2,500 engravings can be found at Twyfelfontein.

BEAD-MAKING – AN ANCIENT TRADITION

Ostrich-eggshell necklaces made by the San are the products of an ancient art, passed on from generation to generation. The eggshells are broken into little pieces, and each fragment is painstakingly rounded with a hard object such as animal horn. Holes are bored through the centre of the flat bead with a blunt metal tip attached to a wooden shaft. To prevent the fragile shell from cracking, the craftsman does not pierce it right through. The remaining outer layer is pierced with a sharp metal point joined to the opposite end of the shaft, thus ensuring a smooth hole. Beads used to be strung onto sinew, but are nowadays threaded together with nylon.

AN ENSEMBLE OF COLOUR AND STYLE

The colourful dress known to the Herero as *ohorokweva* draws its inspiration from the clothing typically worn in the early 1900s by the wives of German missionaries in Namibia. Requiring up to 12 m of dress material, it has long sleeves and prominent shoulders and is taken in above the waist. The dress is worn over petticoats which make it fan out and accentuate the graceful walking style of its owner. A shawl is worn over the shoulders and an apron completes the ensemble. A Herero woman is not fully clothed unless she wears the *otjikaeva* headdress, often matching the colours of her dress. Accessories typically include strings of sweet-smelling wooden beads carved from tamboti wood, known as *otupapa*, and modern jewellery such as rings, bangles and brooches.

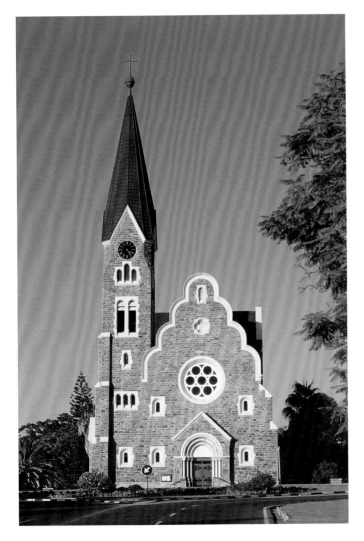

CHRISTUSKIRCHE –

WINDHOEK

The beautiful Christuskirche, or Christ Church, was designed by the architect Gottlieb Redecker. The Evangelical Lutheran Church was constructed between 1907 and 1910 as a symbol of peace after the conclusion of bitter wars between the German colonial administration and the Herero and Nama people. Built of local sandstone, the graceful building displays a mix of architectural influences, including art nouveau, neo-Romanesque and neo-Gothic styles. As with the Evangelical Lutheran churches in Lüderitz and Swakopmund, the stained-glass altar windows adorning the Christuskirche were donated by Kaiser Wilhelm II.

'DAMARA DISCO' IN THE HEART OF THE CITY

Windhoek's music venues, clubs and bars come alive on Friday nights when locals and visitors alike relax to the sounds of the capital's numerous music groups. Some, like the 'Life Boys' (a pun on the name of a well-known brand of soap), hone their skills on city streets, to the delight of appreciative passersby who stop to watch, listen and tap their feet to the group's homegrown 'Damara disco' and gospel music. Namibian music, a rich fusion of local, African and Western styles, is enriched by the indigenous sounds of traditional and homemade instruments.

NAMIBIAN
BASKETRY

The ancient craft of basketry is widely practised in northern Namibia. Wares are produced both for the tourist market and for use in local farming communities, where, for example, baskets and trays are still used to carry crops and winnow grain. The baskets are made from makalani palm leaves, some of which may be dyed with vegetable dyes. The most widely used dye comes from the bark of the bird plum tree, which is boiled with the palm leaves to create a brown colour. The characteristics of baskets change with each region. While baskets from the Okavango region tend to be quite big, those from the Caprivi are often smaller with finer coils. Making baskets is a slow process – some can take as long as four weeks to complete and it takes many years of practice to master the craft.

21

AFRICAN ELEGANCE

Intricately braided and styled with flair, Justina's *coiffure* is the epitome of northern Namibian chic. A member of the Kwambi tribe, she works in a general dealer shop next to the Oshikuku market, where fine examples of local crafts are on display. Meaning 'place of the chicken' or 'chicken coop', Oshikuku is in Namibia's Omusati region.

WATCHING NAMIBIA VERSUS MOZAMBIQUE

With intense focus, these soccer fans are apparently oblivious to the photographer in their midst as they watch Namibia versus Mozambique on outdoor television in September 1998. Mozambique was leading 1–0 at first. Then, in the dying minutes of the game, Namibia snatched a dramatic equaliser before scoring the winning goal, to the nation's delight and jubilation.

MAKALANI PALM

SUNSET

The sight of makalani palms silhouetted against a 'fireball' African sunset is an evocative and indelible image. The palm trees add an exotic touch to the northern Namibian landscape, but they also have a practical value. The fruit have a sweet, juicy outer pulp that provides food for both people and animals. The sap, when tapped and fermented, becomes a popular – and highly intoxicating – liquor. Besides providing invaluable shade, the palms' fronds are skillfully woven into distinctive basketware. Once made primarily for domestic use, baskets of all shapes and sizes are now sold at roadside stalls to appreciative tourists and are exported far beyond Namibia's borders. The makalani palms yield vegetable ivory, or ivory nuts, which offer carvers an environmentally-friendly substitute for elephant ivory.

ETOSHA NATIONAL PARK

The Etosha National Park in northern Namibia is a unique wildlife park, with wide, flat, chalky and desolate plains, shimmering with terrestrial heat. With uninterrupted views as far as the eye can see, the 22,270-square-kilometre park is home to some 144 mammal species, including lion, leopard, cheetah, elephant, giraffe and zebra. Etosha also hosts about 340 bird species, including Namibia's national bird, the crimsonbreasted shrike. The park originally formed part of a network of reserves, known as Game Reserves One, Two and Three, which were proclaimed in 1907 by Governor Friedrich von Lindequist of the German colonial government.

ETOSHA – A WILDLIFE SANCTUARY

During the sweltering heat of the midday sun, a large group of game gathers around a waterhole. This time of the day is most popular amongst the thirsty animals as they are relatively safe from predators who rest to escape the noonday heat. However, the animals remain vigilant, with some appearing to keep watch while others drink. Etosha's waterholes support a rich diversity of mammals and birds, including rare and endangered species such as the black-faced impala, the roan, the black rhinoceros and Namibia's smallest antelope, the Damara dik-dik. Research on Etosha's waterholes has shown that different animals have different preferred drinking times.

LIONS OF NAMIBIA

Namibia's 'king of beasts' surveys his domain in Etosha. The most sociable members of the cat family, lions live in prides, sometimes comprising as many as 50 animals. While the females stealthily hunt with purposeful poise and a powerful pounce, the larger, dominant males defend their territories and prides against invaders and predators. Lions spend most of the day resting, but respond swiftly and ferociously when provoked. Namibia's lions roam Etosha's salt pans, stalk unsuspecting seals on the vast, sandy coastline in the northwest and hunt in Kaokoveld and in the Kalahari Desert next to the Kgalagadi Transfrontier Park.

NOCTURNAL OVERTURE – KAVANGO RIVER

At the end of the day, the twilight colours of burnished gold and silver shimmer on the water. In an overture of the night, rasping insects and croaking frogs are residents in concert.

MEDICINE MAN –
EASTERN CAPRIVI

Adorned with hundreds of clattering bamboo beads, this medicine man practises in Lizauli village in eastern Caprivi. During healing ceremonies ancestral spirits are summoned with the aid of ritual objects and trance dancing. In addition, advice is given and *muti* (traditional medicine) is dispensed to the sick and troubled. The Caprivi, a curious relic of colonialism, extends as a thin sliver of land into the heart of Africa and borders Zimbabwe, Angola, Zambia and Botswana. The Mafwe and Masubia tribes live east of the Kwando River and the Mbukushu live along the banks of the Kavango River in the west. Stretching some 480 km from east to west, the Caprivi Strip is only 32 km wide in some places.

'DESERT'

ELEPHANTS

These remarkable 'desert' elephants migrate along centuries-old 'elephant highways', covering vast distances across the Namib's northern gravel plains. In the Kunene region they are usually found along drainage lines or in riverbeds where they search for food and scarce, but vital, surface water. By the start of the 20th century, Namibia's elephant population was on the brink of extinction. Since then, the introduction of hunting laws, the establishment of game parks and the implementation of conservation policies have helped protect the mammoth pachyderms from exploitation by commercial hunters and poachers. Their numbers have slowly increased and by the mid-1990s there were an estimated 8,000 elephants in Namibia.

THE KUNENE RIVER

The perennial Kunene River rises in the Angolan highlands and enters Namibia at Ruacana Falls where it drops 100 m into a gorge before striking out westward toward the Atlantic Ocean. From Ruacana, the Kunene flows through awesome mountainous terrain: first, through the Zebra Mountains, a geological gem of alternating bands of black granite and dry bush, down Epupa Falls, and then through the gorges and canyons of the Baynes and Ojihipa ranges where, constricted by towering cliffs, the river becomes virtually inaccessible. It then placidly skirts the northern rim of the Marienfluss before continuing its watery ramble through the Hartmann Mountains and across the Namib Desert.

KAOKOVELD – HOME OF THE HIMBA

Himba women from the Ohungumure village in the Kaokoveld wear traditional leather skirts consisting of a larger skin (*oruheke*) at the back and a smaller one at the front. The waistband, made of iron beads, indicates that a woman has had more than one child. The thick shell necklaces signify that a woman is married and has children. Some say the Kaokoveld, in Namibia's remote northwestern corner, is the subcontinent's 'last wilderness'. A vast, rugged and almost impenetrable territory, it is bounded by undulating hills in the south and forbidding mountains in the north. In the east, it is flanked by sandy plains and in the west by a coastal desert. Stretching across about 4,9 million ha between the Kunene and Hoanib rivers, it is sparsely populated – population density averages one person to every two square kilometres.

The *ekori*, with its leather saturated with butterfat and red ochre, is an ornate head-dress, richly decorated with iron beads and worn by adult women at special ceremonial occasions. A prized posses-sion, after a woman's death it will be passed on to her sister or eldest daughter. In the past the large white or speckled conches (*ohumba*) were traded for oxen with the Mbundu and other Angolan tribes. Today the cherished pieces of jewellery are handed down from mother to daughter.

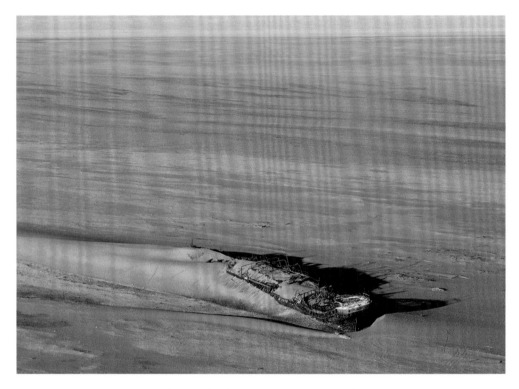

STRANDED IN A SEA OF SAND

In 1910 the *Eduard Bohlen*, a vessel owned by the Hamburg-based Woermann Line, foundered on a sandbank near Conception Bay while on a voyage to deliver supplies to the diamond camps in the Namib Desert. In the absence of a port at the time, supply ships dropped anchor in Conception Bay and transferred their loads into rowing boats. Oarsmen braved pounding waves and buffeting winds to ferry the goods ashore. From there, the cargo was loaded onto ox-wagons and carted several kilometres through the desert to the diamond diggers' settlements. Today, the *Eduard Bohlen* lies marooned in a shallow, sandy grave approximately 300 m inland from the present shore.

THE MEETING OF TWO SEAS

The meeting between sand and sea along Namibia's desert coastline is abrupt and ruthless. As the Atlantic's pounding breakers crash into a wall of sand they truncate the golden waves of the dune sea, creating narrow, confined beaches, sometimes less than a metre wide. The excess sand, as well as sand blown into the ocean by blustery winds, is swept northwards by the icy Benguela Current and deposited along the Skeleton Coast. Together, sea and sand create an ever-changing shoreline – which explains why many shipwrecks are found so far inland.

CAPE FUR SEALS

The Cape fur seal is one of three species of fur seal found in the Southern Ocean, the others being the Antarctic fur seal and the sub-Antarctic fur seal. Two-thirds of the Cape fur seal population are found along the west coast of Namibia where they can be seen in large numbers, snorting and cavorting, belching and bellowing in the surf and on the shore. The colony at Cape Cross Seal Reserve, north of Swakopmund, fluctuates seasonally between 80,000 and 100,000. Pups are usually born during November and December. On average, one out of every four will die in infancy, preyed upon mainly by the black-backed jackal and brown hyena. When they're not playing in the waves or diving for food, they take time out to bask on sandy beaches or rocky outcrops.